4

Essential
Music Theory

Mark Sarnecki

San Marco
Publications

ISNB: 9781896499291

Contents

1

Music Notation

Music existed for a long time before it was written down. Initially it was handed down by rote, which means melodies and songs were taught from generation to generation. There was no written music; people just copied the sounds. Some people still learn music this way. Developing a system of notating music meant that it could be shared far away. It could be played or sung by a musician who could read the lines and symbols created by someone they have never met. In this lesson, we are going to review some of the basic rules of music notation.

The Staff

A single staff never has a left barline. A ***double barline*** at the end of a measure or line indicates the end of a section. It is used to clarify the end of a section such as a ***da capo*** section. Note that the key signature is placed between the clef and the time signature.

Figure 1.1

The grand staff begins with a ***systemic barline***. A systemic barline joins two or more staves together. It goes through both staves to create the grand staff. The grand staff also begins with a brace in front of the systemic barline. A ***final double barline*** at the end consists of a thin line and a thick line. This marks the end of a composition or the end of a movement of a larger work.

Figure 1.2

Notes and Note Stems

Notes are placed on the lines and in the spaces. The normal length of a single stem is usually one octave (3½ spaces). Flags for eighth and sixteenth notes always go on the right side of the note. Groups of eighth or sixteenth notes are joined with beams.

Figure 1.3

Stem Direction for Beamed Groups

Notes below the middle line have stems that go up, and notes above the middle line have stems that go down. Stems of notes on the middle line can go either way.

For two beamed notes, stem direction is determined by the note that is farthest away from the middle line as shown in Figure 1.4. If the note is farther above, the stems go down. If it is farther below, the stems go up.

Figure 1.4

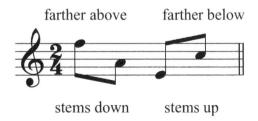

For groups of three or more beamed notes if the majority of notes are **on or above** the middle line the stems go down as in Figure 1.5 a and b. If the majority of the notes are **below** the middle line the stems go up (Figure 1.5 c). If the number of notes **above and below the middle line are equal**, the note farthest from the middle line dictates the stem direction (Figure 1.5 d).

Figure 1.5

Rests

Placement of rests on the staff is important. The whole rest (Figure 1.6 a) is used to indicate a whole measure of rest. It hangs from the fourth line and is placed in the center of the measure. The half rest (Figure 1.6 b) is placed on top of the third line. The quarter rest is positioned as shown in Figure 1.6 c. The bottom hook of this rest goes through the second staff line. The hook of the eight rest is placed in the third space (Figure 1.6 d). The two hooks of the sixteenth rest are placed in the second and third space of the staff. (Figure 1.6 e).

Figure 1.6

Music Notation

1. Add stems to the following note heads.

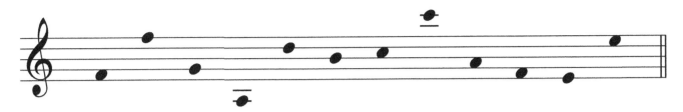

2. Add stems to the following groups of four eighth notes.

3. Circle any notes or groups of notes that have wrong stem direction.

Music Notation

Ledger Lines

Ledger lines are used to extend the range of the staff. Ledger lines are spaced the same distance vertically as the lines of the staff.

Figure 1.7

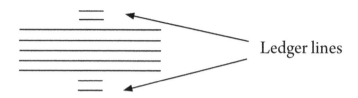

Stems of all notes above and below the first ledger line must extend to the middle staff line (Figure 1.8).

Figure 1.8

Figure 1.9 shows ledger line notes above and below the treble staff.

Figure 1.9

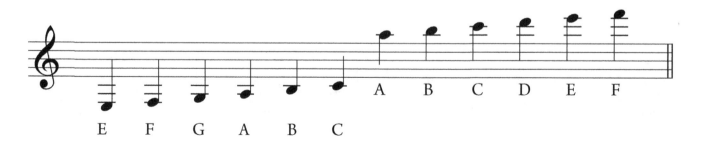

Music Notation

Figure 1.10 shows ledger line notes on the bass staff.

Figure 1.10

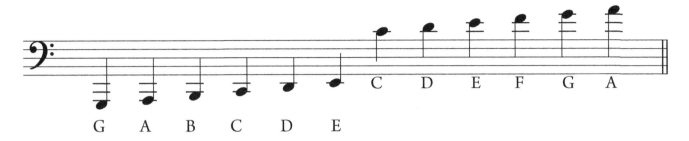

1. Rewrite the following melody in the treble clef at the same pitch.

Mikhail Glinka
Souvenir of a Night in Madrid

2. Rewrite the following melody in the bass clef at the same pitch.

Wolfgang Amadeus Mozart
Piano Concerto K270

Music Notation

2

Time 1

Simple Time Review

Previous levels covered the time signatures 2/4, 3/4, and 4/4. The bottom number of the time signature tells us that the quarter note receives one beat and the top number tells us how many beats are in each measure. Time signatures with 2, 3, or 4 as the top number are in ***simple time***.

Figure 2.1

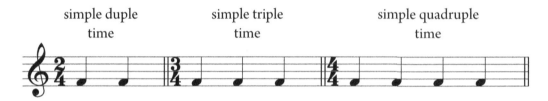

Chart of Relative Note Values

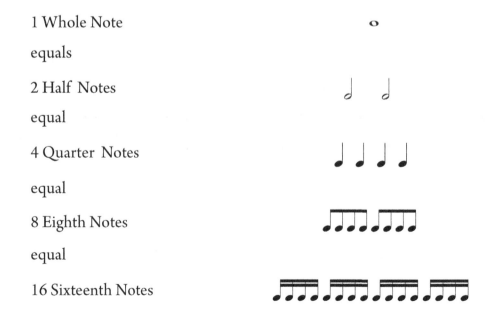

1 Whole Note

equals

2 Half Notes

equal

4 Quarter Notes

equal

8 Eighth Notes

equal

16 Sixteenth Notes

1. Add one note to complete each measure.

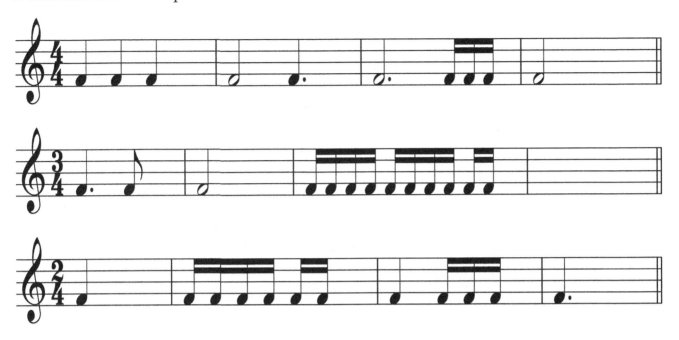

2. Add time signatures at the beginning of each line.

Time 1

The Triplet

When the beat is divided into three equal parts the result is a *triplet*. Triplets fall into a category of notes we call *tuplets*. A tuplet is a group of notes that do not follow the normal rules of counting. In this lesson, we are going to cover triplets.

The Eighth Note Triplet

The most common triplets are eighth note triplets. The three notes of this triplet are beamed together and there is a small "3" over the beam indicating that it is a triplet. This triplet often occurs in 2/4, 3/4, and 4/4 time where it represents one complete beat. Figure 2.2 contains eighth note triplets. When writing eighth note triplets, the number must be positioned avoiding staff lines if possible. The number is placed in the middle of the beam no matter what the stem direction.

Figure 2.2

Triplets are played in the time of two notes of the same value. An eighth note triplet consists of three eighth notes played in the time of two eighth notes. In this case, one beat. Essentially, an eighth note triplet is equal to a quarter note or one beat in quarter time (2/4, 3/4, 4/4). Figure 2.3 shows triplet eighth notes with counting.

Figure 2.3

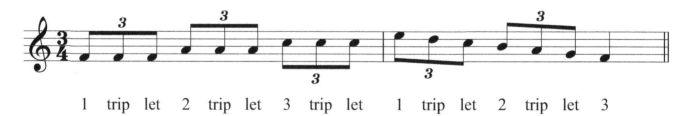

1 trip let 2 trip let 3 trip let 1 trip let 2 trip let 3

1. Add bar lines according to the time signatures.

2. Add time signatures to the following

Robert Schumann
Papillons Op. 2, No. 11

Joseph Haydn
Quartet, Op. 76, No. 5

Antonin Dvorak
Quartet in F

Ludwig van Beethoven
Symphony No. 5, III

Time 1

3
Major Scales

Key Signatures

The first level of organization in a piece of music is the key. Music that uses a key signature is considered **tonal music**. Tonal music is centered around a specific tone called the **tonic**. A piece in C major is a tonal piece centered around the note C, the tonic.

A key signature is used to indicate the sharps or flats that are going to be played throughout a piece of music. Key signatures correspond to major and minor scales. We are going to study key signatures up to three sharps and three flats.

Not just any sharp or flat can appear in a key signature. Sharps and flats are placed in a specific order in a key signature. Here is the order of the first three sharps as they appear in a key signature:

F C G.

Figure 3.1 contains the key signatures up to three sharps on the grand staff.

Figure 3.1

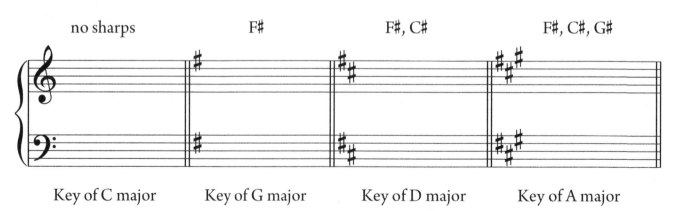

11

1. Write the following key signatures on the grand staff.

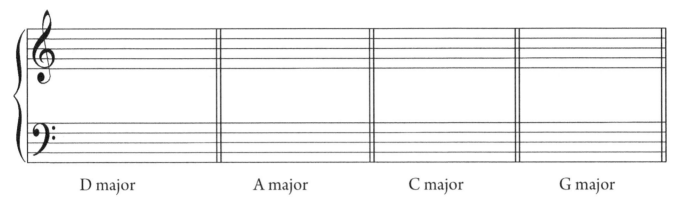

D major   A major   C major   G major

The order of the first three flats as they appear in a key signature is: **B E A.**

Like sharps, flats always appear in a specific order. If there is one flat in a key signature it is always B♭. If there are two flats in a key signature they are always B♭ and E♭. Three = B♭, E♭, A♭, etc. You would never have a key signature with just a A♭. If you have an A♭, There must also be a B♭ and an E♭.

Figure 3.2 contains the key signatures up to three flats on the grand staff.

Figure 3.2

no flats   B♭   B♭, E♭   B♭, E♭, A♭

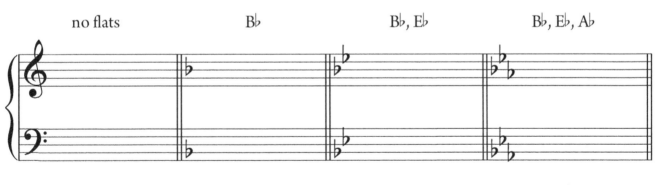

Key of C major   Key of F major   Key of B♭ major   Key of E♭ major

2. Write the following key signatures on the grand staff.

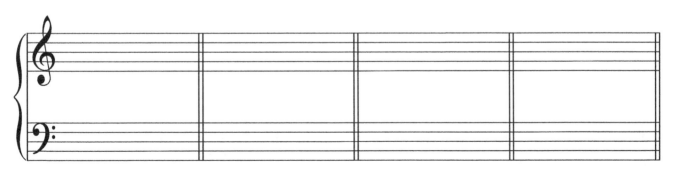

C major   E♭ major   B♭ major   F major

Major Scales

Major Scale Review

A major scale is a series of seven notes (eight with the repeated octave) that has a specific pattern of intervals. It starts and ends on the same note, the tonic. The tonic names the scale. If it starts and ends on G, the tonic is G, and it is the G major scale. Let's review the order of intervals in the major scale. Major scales are built on the following pattern of whole steps and half steps:

whole step - whole step - half step - whole step - whole step - whole step - half step

The scale can also be divided into two four note sections called tetrachords as shown in Figure 3.3. Each tetrachord is WWH with a W between the two (WWH W WWH).

Scale tones can be labeled with a number and a small sign called a **caret** on top ($\hat{1}$, $\hat{2}$, etc.). This indicates a **scale degree**. The first note of a scale is scale degree one ($\hat{1}$), The second is scale degree two ($\hat{2}$), etc.

Figure 3.3

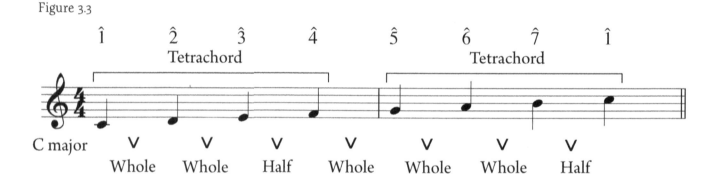

Figure 3.4 contains the A major scale ascending and descending written two different ways. The first uses accidentals instead of a key signature. The second uses a key signature.

Figure 3.4

A major

A major

1. Write the following scales ascending and descending using whole notes and a key signature.

A major

D major

C major

G major

A major

Major Scales

Technical Names for Scale Degrees

Each scale degree can have a technical name. This is a list of the names for four of the scale degrees covered in previous levels.

$\hat{1}$ tonic
$\hat{4}$ subdominant
$\hat{5}$ dominant
$\hat{7}$ leading tone

1. Write the following scales in half notes ascending and descending using a key signature. Label the tonic (T) and dominant (D) notes.

F major

B♭ major

C major

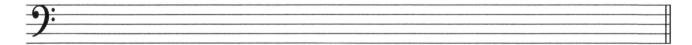

E♭ major

Major Scales

2. For the following scales: Add clefs and accidentals to create major scales. Label the leading tone(LT) for each. Do not duplicate scales.

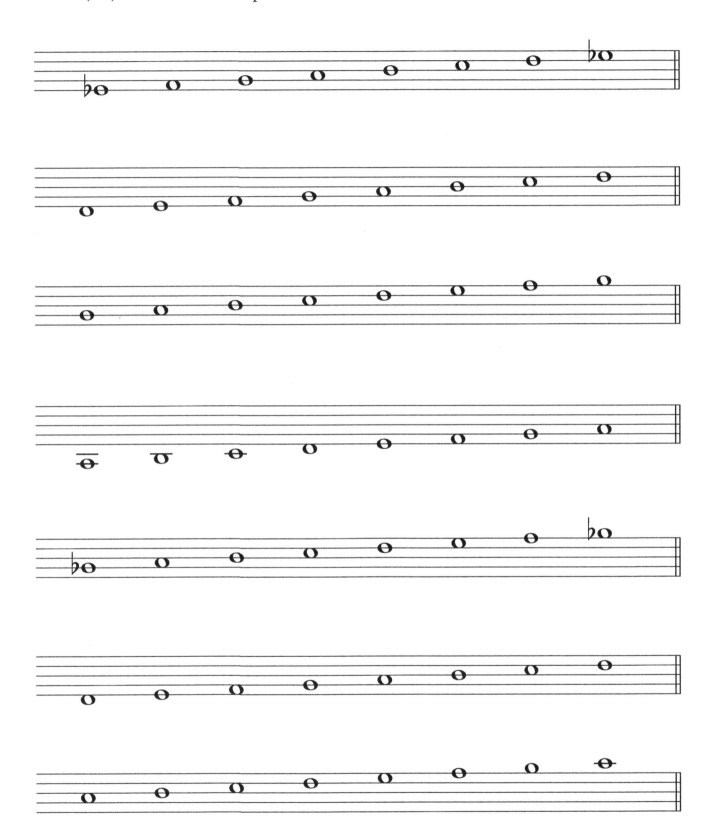

Major Scales

3. Write the following scales in quarter notes ascending and descending using key signatures.

The major scale with 3 sharps

The major scale with 3 flats

The major scale with 2 flats

The major scale with F♯ as its leading tone

The major scale with A as its dominant

The major scale with F as its subdominant

4
History 1

The Orchestra

An **orchestra** is a large group of musicians playing various instruments. The orchestra is lead by the **conductor**. It is divided into groups of related instruments called **sections**. The four main sections of the orchestra are:

- Strings
- Woodwinds
- Brass
- Percussion

Strings

String instruments use vibrating strings to make sound. The strings are stretched across the hollow body of the instrument and plucked or played with a bow. The string section consists of:

- Violins
- Violas
- Cellos
- Double basses
- Harp

Woodwinds

Woodwind instruments consist of long hollow tubes of wood or metal. The player creates sound by blowing air through a thin piece of shaved wood called a 'reed' or blowing across a mouthpiece. Finger holes on the instruments are open and closed to change the pitch. The woodwind section consists of:

- Clarinets
- Flutes and Piccolos
- Oboes
- Bassoons and Double Bassoons
- Saxophones

Brass

Brass instruments are wind instruments made of metal with a cup-shaped mouthpiece. The player creates sound by pressing his or her lips together in the mouthpiece and pushing air out as if they were making a buzzing sound. This creates a vibrating column of air inside the instrument and produces sound. The brass section is made up of:

- Horns
- Trumpets
- Trombones
- Tubas

Percussion

Percussion instruments are instruments that are played by being struck or shaken. There are many percussion instruments. Some create specific pitches like the marimba, xylophone, and the timpani. These are some of the instruments of the percussion section:

- Bass drum
- Chimes
- Gong
- Triangle
- Cymbals
- Snare drum
- Tambourine
- Drum
- Timpani
- Xylophone
- Marimba

Figure 4.1 is a standard seating chart for an orchestra.

Figure 4.1

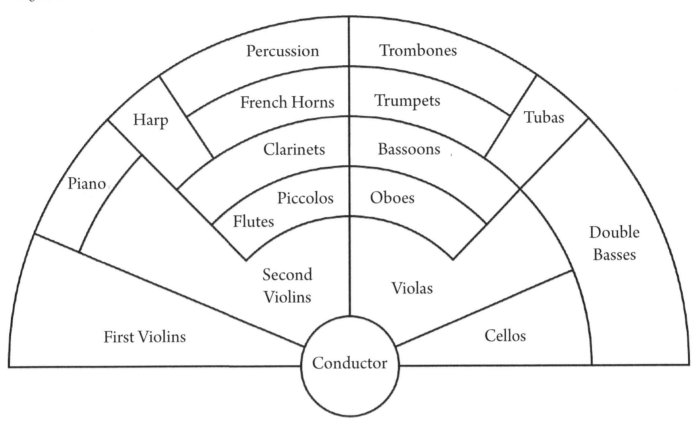

Music Terms

Review the following musical terms from Levels 1 to 4 that are related to style.

cantabile	in a singing style
dolce	sweetly
grazioso	gracefully
maestoso	majestically
marcato	marked or stressed

Review 1

1. Add stems to the following groups of four eighth notes.

2. Rewrite the following melody in the treble clef at the same pitch.

Claude Debussy
Prelude "Voiles"

3. Add barlines according to the time signatures

4. Add one rest to complete each measure.

5. Add the time signature at the beginning of each line.

Review 1

6. Write the following key signatures on the grand staff.

B♭ major   D major   E♭ major   A major

7. Write the following scales in whole notes ascending and descending using a key signature.

The major scale with C♯ as its leading tone

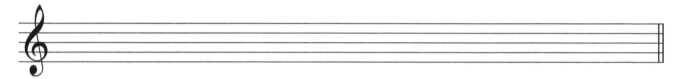

The major scale with E as its dominant

The major scale with A♭ as its subdominant

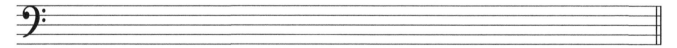

The major scale with B♭ as its tonic

8. Name the four instrument families of the orchestra and name three instruments in each instrument family.

1._____

    a.   _____

    b.   _____

    c.   _____

2._____

    a.   _____

    b.   _____

    c.   _____

3._____

    a.   _____

    b.   _____

    c.   _____

4._____

    a.   _____

    b.   _____

    c.   _____

9. Define the following music terms.

cantabile   _____

dolce   _____

grazioso   _____

maestoso   _____

marcato   _____

5
Minor Scales

There are three types of minor scales: ***natural minor, harmonic minor***, and ***melodic minor***. Each of these minor scales has a different order of whole and half steps. Thankfully, it is not necessary to memorize these patterns to study minor scales.

Relative Major and Minor Keys

Major and minor scales are related by key signature. Every major key has a relative minor. They are related because they share the same key signature. C major and A minor have no sharps or flats. C major is the relative major of A minor and vice versa.

To determine a minor key signature:

1. Name the major key.

2. Count up six notes (or down three) to get the relative minor key.

The 6th note of the G major scale is E. E minor has the same key signature as G major, one sharp, F♯. Every key signature reflects two keys, one major and one minor.

Figure 5.1

G major scale

E natural minor scale

Minor Scales

Figure 5.2 is a chart of the relative major and minor keys up to three sharps and three flats.

Figure 5.2

Sharp Keys	Major	Minor
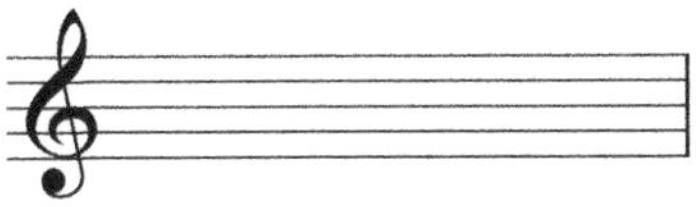	C	A
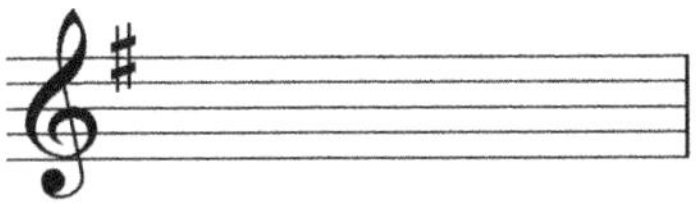	G	E
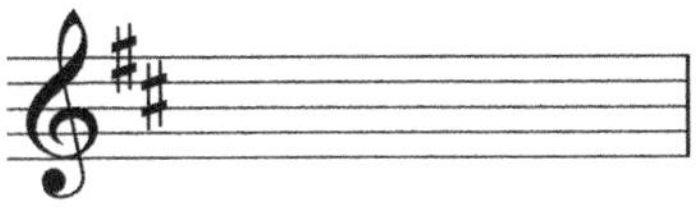	D	B
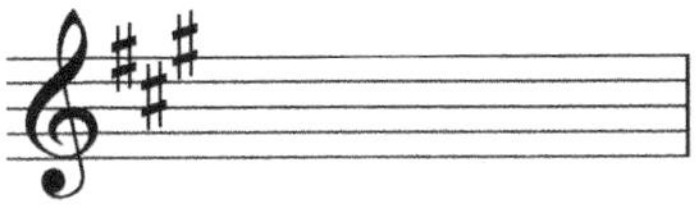	A	F♯

Flat Keys	Major	Minor
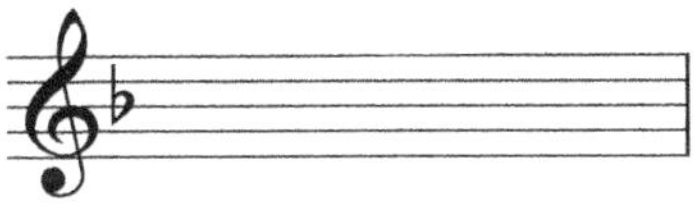	F	D
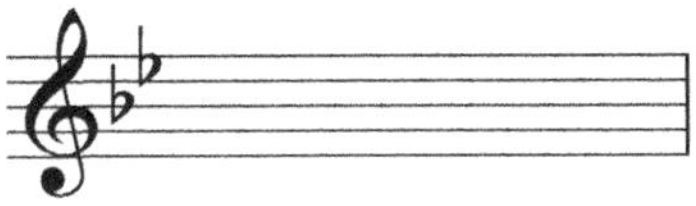	B♭	G
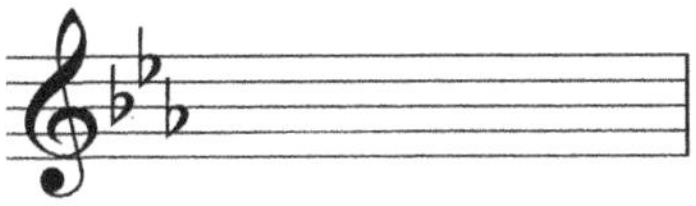	E♭	C

1. Name the relative major or minor key of the following:

D minor _____   B♭ major _____

E minor _____   C major _____

B minor _____   D major _____

C minor _____   E♭ major _____

F# minor _____   A major _____

Parallel Major and Minor Keys

Major and minor keys that share the same root or tonic are considered *parallel major and minor keys*. Sometimes they are called *tonic major and minor*. C major and C minor are parallel major and minor or tonic major and minor. This means they share the same tonic. Here are the notes of the C major scale:

C D E F G A B C

Here are the notes of the C natural minor scale:

C D E♭ F G A♭ B♭ C

The difference between these scales is three notes. From C major to C minor, three notes have been lowered to flats: E, A and B have been lowered to E♭, A♭ and B♭. In other words, $\hat{3}$, $\hat{6}$, and $\hat{7}$ have been lowered one half step to create the natural minor scale. This applies to all keys. If you lower $\hat{3}$, $\hat{6}$, and $\hat{7}$ of any major scale you get its parallel minor.

As we move through music theory studies we will see that many things can be derived from a major scale. This is simply another way to find the parallel minor scale.

Minor Scales

Minor Scale Review

These are the three versions of the minor scale:

- The **natural minor scale** is the minor scale without any altered notes.
- The **harmonic minor scale** has raised $\hat{7}$ ascending and descending.
- The **melodic minor scale** has $\hat{6}$ and $\hat{7}$ raised ascending and lowered descending.

Figure 5.3 illustrates all three versions of the A minor scale.

Figure 5.3

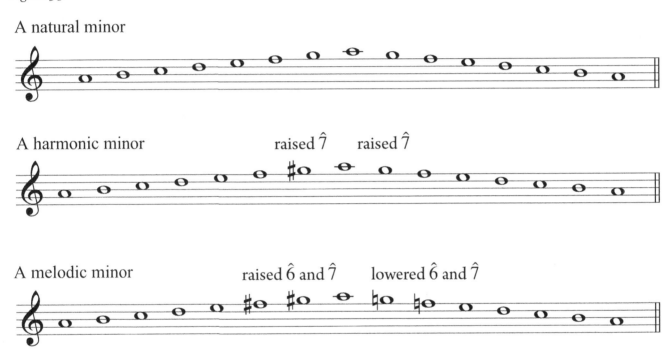

The Leading Tone Versus The Subtonic

Most of the time, minor keys require raised $\hat{7}$ in order for them to work harmonically in a composition. When we raise $\hat{7}$ it becomes a half step away from the tonic and this gives it a natural pull to the tonic. This is why it is called the **leading tone**. It "leads" to the tonic.

If $\hat{7}$ is not raised, as in the natural minor scale, or the descending melodic minor scale, it does not have this pull to the tonic and is not called the leading tone. In this case it is a called the **subtonic**. The subtonic only occurs in a minor key. In A minor, G♯ is the leading tone and G♮ is the subtonic. In major keys, there is no subtonic because $\hat{7}$ is always a semitone away from the tonic and it is always called the leading tone.

1. Write the following scales ascending and descending in whole notes using key signatures. Label the leading tone (LT) and the subtonic (ST) where applicable.

B natural minor

B harmonic minor

B melodic minor

G natural minor

G harmonic minor

G melodic minor

Minor Scales

2. Identify the following minor scales.

_____

_____

_____

_____

_____

_____

_____

Minor Scales

3. Write the following scales ascending and descending using a key signature in quarter notes.

G harmonic minor

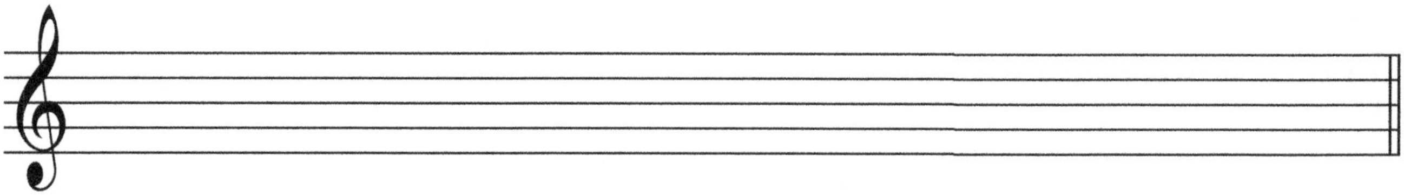

A natural minor

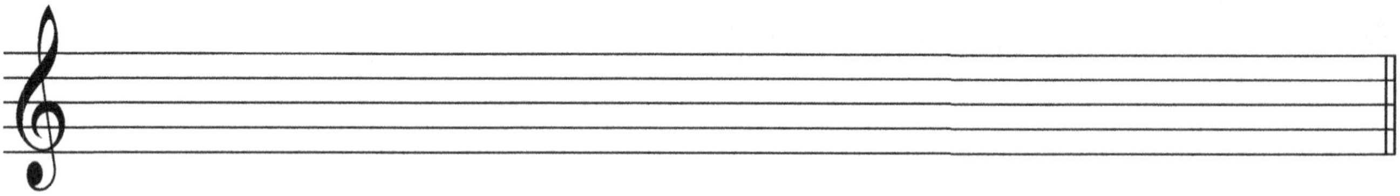

C melodic minor

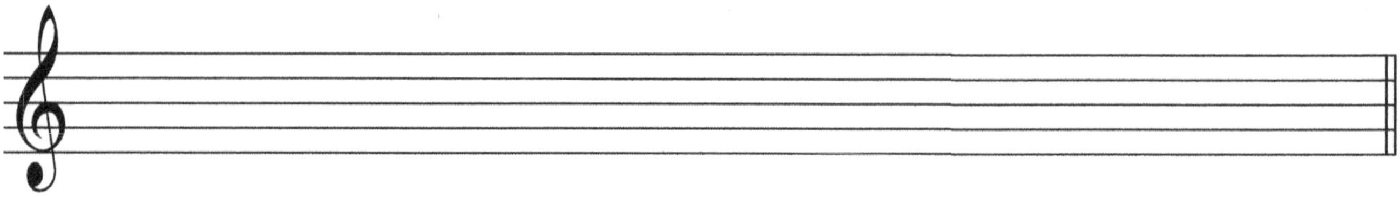

E harmonic minor

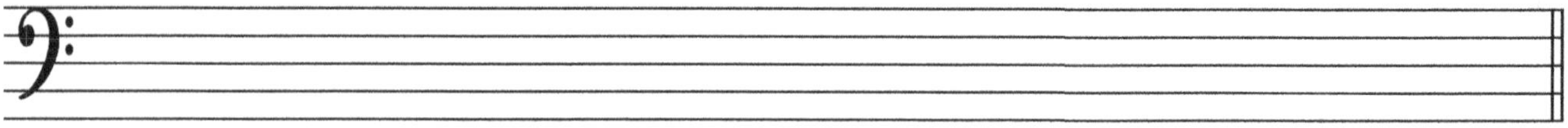

F# melodic minor

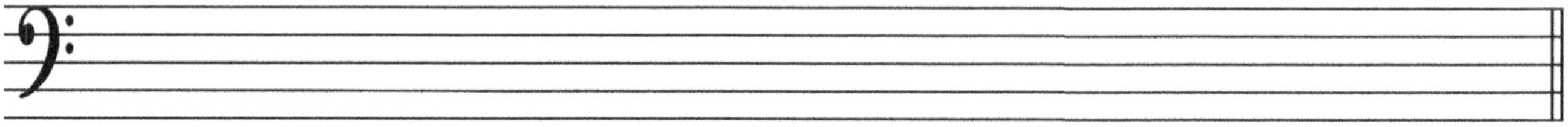

D natural minor

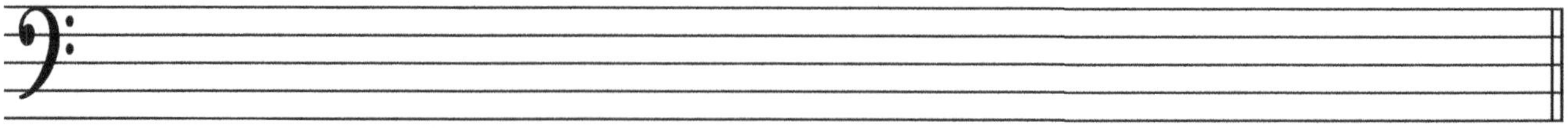

B harmonic minor

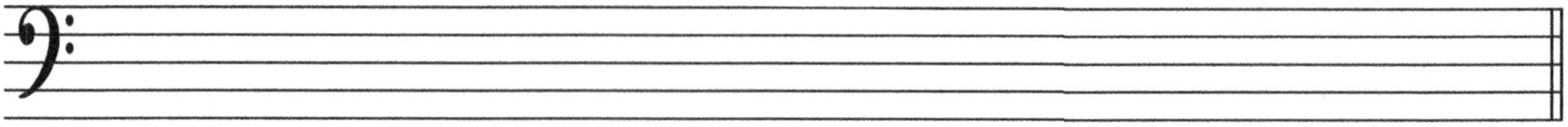

Minor Scales

6
Intervals

We use whole and half steps to understand the structure of scales. These are *intervals*. In music, the term interval refers to the distance between two notes. An interval consists of two elements: numeric size and quality or type. Understanding the interval is essential to understanding music theory.

Major Intervals

Major intervals only occur on the following numbers: 2, 3, 6, and 7. In order for an interval to be major it must be one of these numbers, and the top note must be a member of the bottom notes major scale.

Figure 6.1 illustrates major intervals on different notes.

a. C to D is a major 2nd because D is the second note of the C major scale.
b. D to F♯ is a major 3rd. F must be sharp since it is the third note of the D major scale. F♮ would not be a major 3rd here.
c. E♭ to C is a major 6th because C is the 6th note of the E♭ major scale.
d. G to B is major 3rd since B is scale degree $\hat{3}$ of the G major scale.
e. D to C♯ is a major 7th since the scale of D major has C♯ as its 7th note.

When you write and solve intervals, the key signature of the bottom notes major scale is crucial. Knowing the key signatures is essential when dealing with intervals.

Figure 6.1

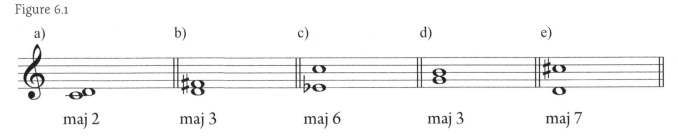

Perfect Intervals

The number of a perfect interval is always 1, 4, 5, or 8. Even though a unison (1) isn't really an interval, since there is no distance between its notes, it is still considered perfect. For an interval to be perfect the top note must be a member of the bottom notes major scale.

Figure 6.2 illustrates a number of perfect intervals. a) is a perfect unison. In b), A♭ is a perfect 4th above E♭ because A♭ is the fourth note of the E♭ major scale. A♮ would not be a perfect 4th here because it is not a member of E♭'s scale. When solving intervals always think of the major scale of the bottom note. Is the top note a member of the bottom notes major scale? If it is, the interval will be perfect, or major depending on the number.

Figure 6.2

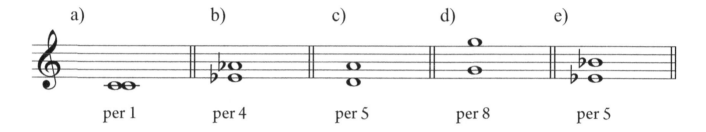

1. Name the following intervals.

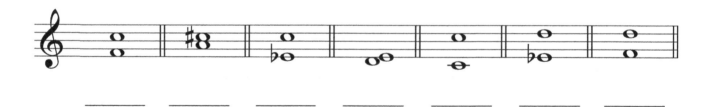

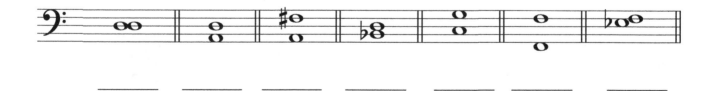

Intervals

Intervals in a Major Scale

Figure 6.3 shows the C major scale with its intervals. The intervals are measured from the root C to the notes above it. The intervals that result are all major or perfect. 2nds, 3rds, 6ths and 7ths are major intervals. Unisons (1s), 4ths, 5th, and octaves (8ths) are perfect intervals.

Figure 6.3

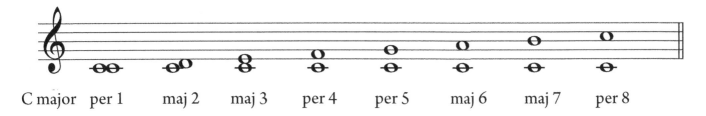

C major   per 1   maj 2   maj 3   per 4   per 5   maj 6   maj 7   per 8

1. Using accidentals write the intervals that occur on the following major scales.

F major

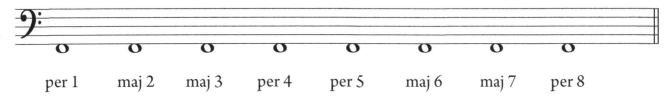

per 1   maj 2   maj 3   per 4   per 5   maj 6   maj 7   per 8

B♭ major

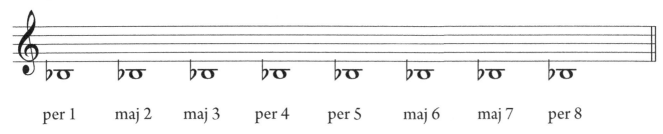

per 1   maj 2   maj 3   per 4   per 5   maj 6   maj 7   per 8

E♭ major

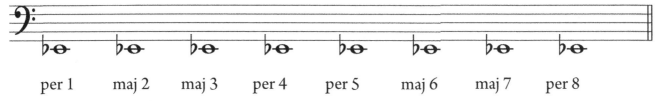

per 1   maj 2   maj 3   per 4   per 5   maj 6   maj 7   per 8

Minor Intervals

Only 2nds, 3rds, 6ths, and 7ths can be ***minor intervals***. They are always a half step smaller or closer together than a major interval that has the same number. A minor 2nd is the smallest interval. The half step is a minor 2nd.

Figure 6.4 shows the differences between major and minor intervals.

a. C to D is a major 2nd, because D is a note of the C major scale. C to D♭ is one half step smaller or closer together and is a minor 2nd. D♭ is not a note of the C major scale.
b. D to F♯ is a major 3rd because F♯ is a note of the D major scale. D to F♮ is a minor 3rd because it is one half step closer together than the major interval D- F♯.
c. F to D is a major 6th because D is the sixth note of the F major scale. F to D♭ is a half step closer together and is a minor 6th.
d. D to C♯ is a major 7th. D to C♮ is a half step closer together so it is a minor 7th.

A minor interval is one half step smaller or closer together than a major interval. Only major intervals (2nds, 3rds, 6ths and 7ths) can become minor intervals. Perfect intervals (1, 4, 5, and 8) never become minor intervals.

Figure 6.4

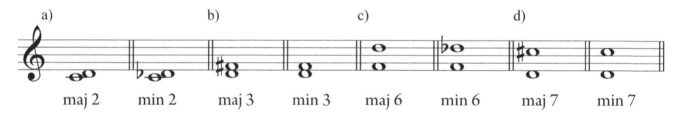

1. Name the following major intervals. Rewrite them making them minor intervals by lowering the top note one half step.

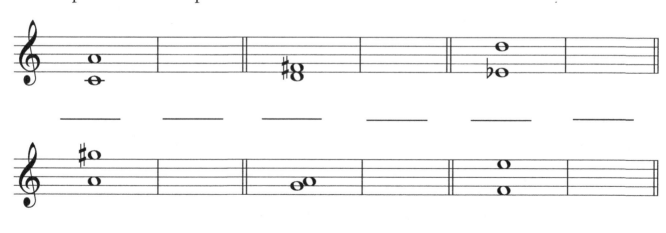

Intervals

Solving Intervals

Use the following steps to solve an intervals number and quality:

1. Count the notes from the bottom up to determine the interval number. Always start by counting the bottom note as 1. In Figure 6.5 A to F is a 6th. A-B-C-D-E-F is 1-2-3-4-5-6.
2. Determine by the number if the interval should be major or perfect. A 6th would be a major interval.
3. Decide if the top note is a member of the bottom notes major scale. Here, F♮ is not a member of the A major scale since A major has an F♯. It has been lowered one half step making this interval a minor 6th.

Figure 6.5

min 6

2. Name the following intervals.

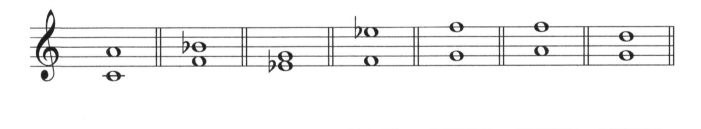

_____   _____   _____   _____   _____   _____   _____

_____   _____   _____   _____   _____   _____   _____

Intervals

3. Write the following harmonic intervals.

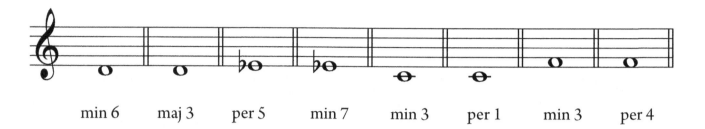

min 6   maj 3   per 5   min 7   min 3   per 1   min 3   per 4

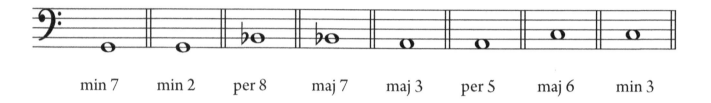

min 7   min 2   per 8   maj 7   maj 3   per 5   maj 6   min 3

4. Write the following harmonic intervals.

per 5   maj 3   min 7   maj 6   min 3   per 1   maj 6   min 6

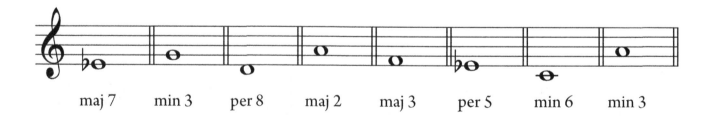

maj 7   min 3   per 8   maj 2   maj 3   per 5   min 6   min 3

Intervals

5. Write the following harmonic intervals.

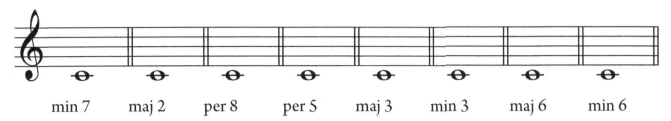

min 7   maj 2   per 8   per 5   maj 3   min 3   maj 6   min 6

min 7   maj 2   per 8   per 5   maj 3   min 3   maj 6   min 6

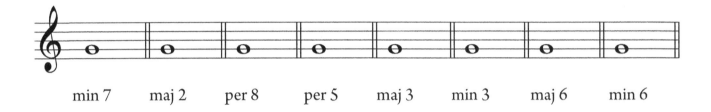

min 7   maj 2   per 8   per 5   maj 3   min 3   maj 6   min 6

min 7   maj 2   per 8   per 5   maj 3   min 3   maj 6   min 6

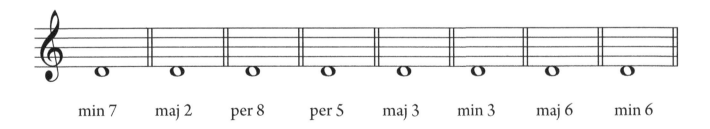

min 7   maj 2   per 8   per 5   maj 3   min 3   maj 6   min 6

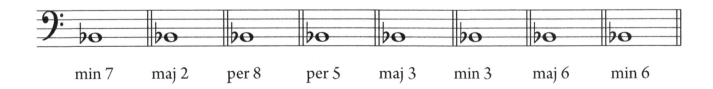

min 7   maj 2   per 8   per 5   maj 3   min 3   maj 6   min 6

Intervals

6. Name the melodic intervals under the brackets.

Johann Strauss
Emperor Waltz

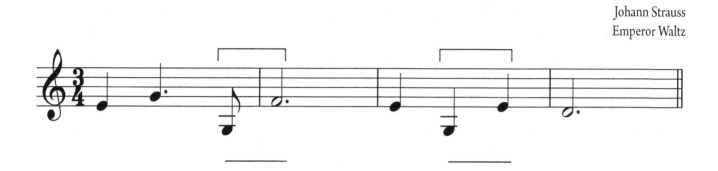

Traditional
All Through the Night

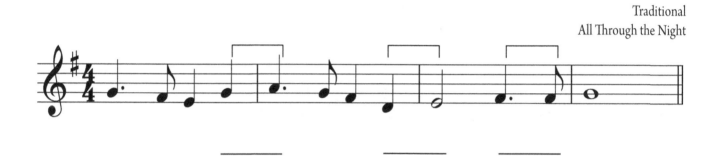

Wofgang Amadeus Mozart
Minuet, K. 3

Johann Sebastian Bach
Passacaglia for Organ

Intervals

7

Octave Transposition

The Octave

An octopus has 8 legs. An octagon has 8 sides. We know from studying intervals than an *octave* is the interval that spans 8 notes.

An octave is from one letter name to the **same** letter name, up or down.

1. Write octaves on the grand staff below.

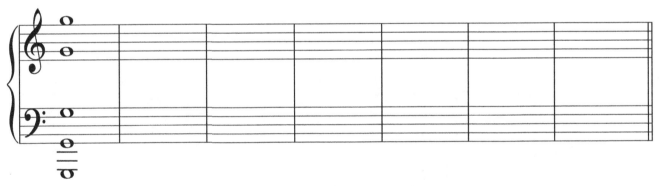

| 5 different | 5 different | 5 different | 5 different | 5 different | 5 different | 5 different |
| Gs | As | Bs | Cs | Ds | Es | Fs |

2. Circle all the octaves found in the example below.

Octave Transposition

Transposition takes place when a group of notes is moved up or down.

In this level we are going to transpose by writing melodies at a different octave.

Figure 7.1 shows a short melody transposed up one octave from the bass staff onto the treble staff.

Figure 7.1

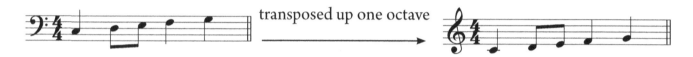

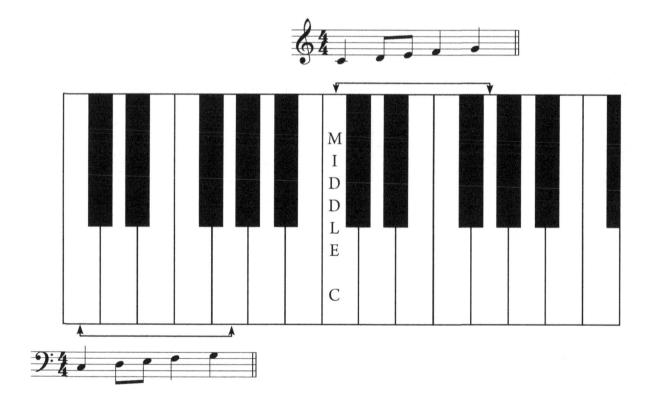

This is not the only way to transpose. Notes on the treble staff may be transposed down into the bass staff.

The melody in Figure 7.2 is transposed down one octave from the treble staff to the bass staff.

When you transpose by an octave:

1. The key remains the same. The clef changes, and the same key signature is used but it is written correctly for the new clef.
2. The time signature remains the same.
3. Every note moves the interval of a perfect octave.
4. The normal rules of stem direction are followed.

The melody in Figure 7.2 requires quite a few ledger line notes on the bass staff to obtain the correct pitch.

Figure 7.2

Francois Couperin
Concerto No. 8

Francois Couperin
Concerto No. 8

1. Transpose the following notes down one octave into the bass clef.

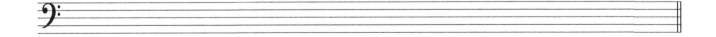

Octave Transposition

2. Transpose the following notes up one octave into the treble clef.

3. Transpose the following melodies up one octave into the treble clef.

Ludwig van Beethoven
Leonore, No. 2

Enrique Granados
Spanish Dance, No. 6

Octave Transposition

4. Transpose the following melodies down one octave into the bass clef.

Johannes Brahms
Seranade in D, V

Frederic Chopin
Nocturne Op. 72, No. 1

Octave Transposition

8

Time 2

More Simple Time Signatures

The time signature 2/8 is in *simple duple time*. The eighth note receives one beat and there are two beats in each measure. In other words, every measure is equal to two eighth notes. Study Figure 8.1.

2
8

two beats in each measure

the eighth note receives one beat

Figure 8.1

1   2   1   2   1   2   1   2

3/8 is a ***simple triple time*** signature. There are three beats in each measure and the eighth note receives one beat. Study Figure 8.2.

3
8

three beats in each measure

the eighth note receives one beat

Figure 8.2

4/8 is a ***simple quadruple time*** signature. There are four beats in each measure and the eighth note receives one beat. Study Figure 8.3.

4
8

four beats in each measure

the eighth note receives one beat

Figure 8.3

1. Add the correct time signature at the beginning of each line.

Time 2

2. Add one note to complete each measure.

The Sixteenth Note Triplet

To determine the length of a sixteenth note triplet we follow the rule that a triplet's length is the same as two notes of the same value. A sixteenth note triplet is three sixteenth notes in the time of two sixteenth notes. This is equal to one eighth note. In 2/8, 3/8, and 4/8 time this means that triplet sixteenth notes are equal to one beat. Figure 8.4 contains triplet sixteenth notes.

Figure 8.4

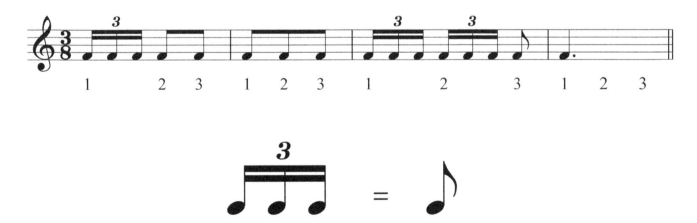

3. Add bar lines according to the time signatures.

Time 2

4. Add one rest to complete each measure according to the time signatures.

Syncopation

A lot of music follows a strict 4/4 tempo or four beats to every measure. The first beat of the measure is a strong beat and it is emphasized. Clap the rhythm of Figure 8.5 and count a steady 4 beats. Clap on each beat emphasizing the first beats. These are steady single beats.

Figure 8.5

Figure 8.6 is a syncopated rhythm. Clap the beats, but hold out beat 4 and don't clap on the next, or first, beat which is tied. Instead emphasize the 2nd beats.

Figure 8.6

Often, the emphasis is given to the first beat of a measure. Syncopation means to shift the typical accent and emphasize what would normally be a "weak" beat. Not playing on the first beat creates a sense of anticipation and gives the music a jazzy feeling. Syncopation can also be created with longer notes in unexpected places as shown in Figure 8.7. Placing a half note on beat two in measure 2 emphasizes a weak beat by holding it longer. This also occurs with the quarter note on the second half of beat three in measure 3.

Figure 8.7

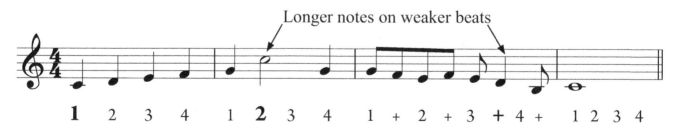

Rests in Simple Time

There are specific rules for adding rests to a measure in simple time. It is important to show each beat as clearly as possible. Each beat or each part of the beat must be completed before beginning the next beat. In Figure 8.8 measure 2, each eighth note beat is finished with an eighth note rest. In measures 3 and 4, the sixteenth note has a sixteenth rest to complete part of the beat and then an eighth rest to finish the remainder of the beat.

Figure 8.8

In Figure 8.9, measure 3, the incomplete sixteenth note beats are completed separately with sixteenth note rests. This shows each beat. Joining these rests into one eighth rest is wrong.

Figure 8.9

In simple triple time each beat or part of the beat should be completed first. Join beats 1 and 2, a strong and weak beat, into one rest. **Do not join beats 2 and 3, two weak beats, into one rest.** Never join two weak beats into one rest.

Figure 8.10

Time 2

We never use rests larger than one beat unless it is in the first half or last half of a measure in simple quadruple time (4/4, 4/8). Join beats 1 and 2 and beats 3 and 4 into one rest. **Never join beats 2 and 3, a weak beat and a medium beat, into one rest.** As in all simple time signatures, finish any incomplete beats first.

Figure 8.11

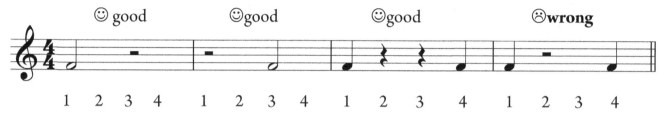

A whole rest represents a complete measure of silence in almost all time signatures.

Figure 8.12

1. Complete the following **single quarter note** beats by adding rests.

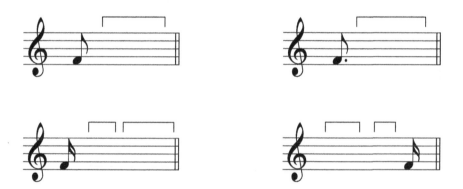

2. Add one rest under each bracket to complete the following measures.

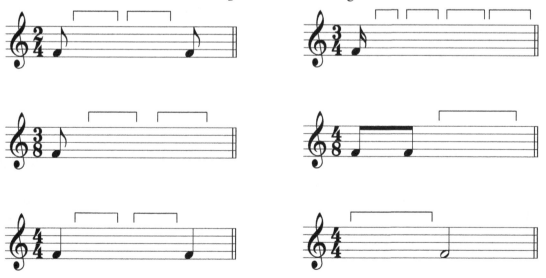

Time 2

3. Add the correct number of rests under each bracket to complete each measure.

Time 2

9
History 2

Benjamin Britten (1913 - 1976) Modern Era

Benjamin Britten was an accomplished conductor, composer, and pianist. He was born in Lowestoft, a town on the English seacoast on November 22nd, the feast day of St. Cecilia, the patron saint of music. Benjamin's mother was a singer and often held concerts in their home.

Britton won a scholarship to the Royal College of Music in London, and his first job was writing music for films.

He did not believe in war and when England decided to go to war with Germany in 1939, Britten left for America. However, he had a great love for the United Kingdom, and in the middle of World War II, he sailed back to his native country.

After the war, the largest opera company in England held a gala and commissioned Britten to write them a new opera.
He also composed an opera to honor the coronation of Queen Elizabeth II. Benjamin Britton was the first musician to be gifted with the title of "Lord" by the Queen.

Young Persons Guide to the Orchestra

The **Young Person's Guide to the Orchestra** is a composition for orchestra written in 1946 by Benjamin Britten. It was initially written for an educational film called *Instruments of the Orchestra* featuring the London Symphony Orchestra. It is one of Britten's best-known compositions.

Young Persons Guide to the Orchestra is based on a piece titled *Rondeau* by the Baroque composer Henry Purcell. The form of Britton's composition is *Theme and Variations*. In this form, the theme is stated first, followed by 13 variations. The variations are short pieces based on the theme that vary in mood and sound. Young Persons Guide to the Orchestra is specifically designed to feature the instruments of the orchestra.

The work begins with the theme (based on Purcell's Rondeau) performed by all the instruments of the orchestra. This is followed by each family of instrument: first the woodwinds, then the brass, then the strings, and finally the percussion. Each variation features an instrument in detail and moves through the family from the highest to the lowest sounding. The first variation starts with piccolos and flutes. Following that, each member of the woodwinds gets a variation including the oboes, the clarinets, and finally the lowest sounding bassoons. The variations then go through the strings, the brass, and ends with the percussion.

After the whole orchestra has played through the instrumental sections (13 variations), all of the instruments join together in the final section to perform a fugue* which starts with the piccolo, followed by the woodwinds, strings, brass, and percussion. Once everyone has entered, the brass section is heard again along with a bang on the gong playing Purcell's original melody. Find a recording of Young Persons Guide to the Orchestra on the internet and listen to it.

*A *fugue* is a composition with two or more voices or parts, in which the melody (called the subject), is played by one voice or part and then replayed and changed by the other voices or parts. Fugues contain between two to five parts.

Music Terms and Signs

Terms

accelerando, accel.	becoming quicker
adagio	slow
prestissimo	as fast as possible
Tempo primo, (Tempo I)	return to the original tempo
vivace	lively, brisk
mano destra, M.D.	right hand
mano sinistra, M.S.	left hand

Signs

⊓	down bow	on a string instrument, play the note by drawing the bow downward
V	up bow	on a string instrument, play the note by drawing the bow upward
,	breath mark	take a breath or a small break

Review 2

1. Write the following scales ascending and descending using a key signature in half notes.

The harmonic minor with F# as the leading tone

The natural minor with G as the dominant

The melodic minor with G as the subdominant

The harmonic minor with the key signature of 3 sharps

The melodic minor with the key signature of 1 sharp

The melodic minor with the key signature of 2 sharps

58

2. Write the following harmonic intervals.

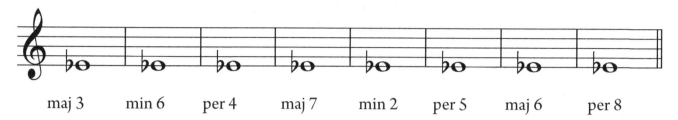

maj 3   min 6   per 4   maj 7   min 2   per 5   maj 6   per 8

3. Write the following melodic intervals.

min 6   min 3   maj 2   min 7   min 2   per 5   maj 6   per 1

4. Name the following intervals.

___   ___   ___   ___   ___   ___   ___

5. Add bar lines according to the time signatures.

6. Add one rest to complete each measure according to the time signatures.

7. Transpose the following melody up one octave into the treble clef.

William Byrd
Pavan

8. Transpose the following melody down one octave into the bass clef.

Felix Mendelssohn
Faith from Song Without Words

Review 2

9. Define the following musical terms.

accelerando _____

adagio _____

mano destra _____

mano sinistra _____

prestissimo _____

Tempo primo _____

vivace _____

10. Answer the following questions.

a. Who composed Young Persons Guide to the Orchestra? _____

b. In what country was he born?_____

c. In what era did he live? _____

d. Who composed the theme on which this work is based? _____

e. What era did this composer live? _____

f. How many variations are in Young Persons Guide to the Orchestra? _____

g. What are the four instrument families featured in this composition?

1. _____

2. _____

3. _____

4. _____

h. What type of piece is the final movement of this composition? _____

10

Chords

A chord consists of three or more notes that are sounded at the same time. Chords may be played by a solo instrument like a piano or a guitar. They may also be played by many instruments at once, like an orchestra or a string quartet. The instruments work together to create chords. Like intervals, there are different qualities of chords. The quality is determined by the intervals that make up the chord. In this level, we will study **major** and **minor triads**.

Major Triads

A triad is a three note chord consisting of a root, third and fifth. Major triads are considered "major" because they are made up of certain intervals.

A major triad consists of a major third and a perfect fifth above the root.

Figure 10.1 contains a major triad built on the root D. There is a major third between D and F♯ and a perfect fifth between D and A. All major triads contain these intervals between the root and third and the root and fifth.

Figure 10.1

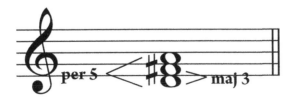

D - F♯ = major 3rd
D - A = perfect 5th

Chords

Triads in Major Keys

In a major key, there are three major triads. They occur when you build triads on $\hat{1}$, $\hat{4}$, and $\hat{5}$ of the major scale. They are considered the tonic, subdominant and dominant triads in a key. Figure 10.2 contains the triads built on these scale degrees in C major. All three are major triads because they consist of a major 3rd and perfect fifth above the root.

Figure 10.2

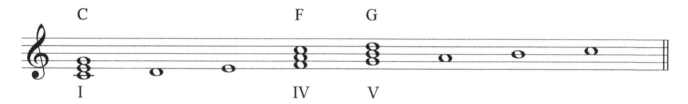

Chord Symbols

We label chords with symbols. A chord can have two symbols. A Roman numeral placed under the chord and a letter name placed above the chord. The Roman numeral is known as a ***functional chord symbol*** and the letter is known as a ***root/quality chord symbol***.

Each Roman numeral corresponds to the scale degree that the chord was built upon. Major triads always receive an uppercase Roman numeral as shown in Figure 10.2.

- The chord built on $\hat{1}$ is the *tonic triad* and it's Roman numeral is **I**.
- The chord built on $\hat{4}$ is the *subdominant triad* and it's Roman numeral is **IV**.
- The chord built on $\hat{5}$ is the *dominant triad* and it's Roman numeral is **V**.

Chords may also have a letter name called the root/quality chord symbol. This name comes from the root of the chord. The letter indicates the root of the chord. The letter written by itself as a capitol letter means that the chord is major.

In C major: The chord built on $\hat{1}$ (C), uses the root/quality chord symbol **C**.
The chord built on $\hat{4}$ (F), uses the root/quality chord symbol **F**.
The chord built on $\hat{5}$ (G), uses the root/quality chord symbol **G**.

1. Write triads on $\hat{1}$, $\hat{4}$, and $\hat{5}$ of the following major scales. Add the functional and the root/quality chord symbols.

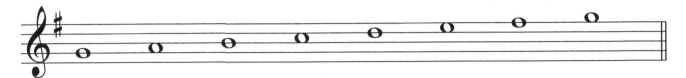

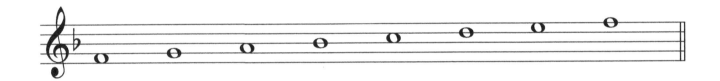

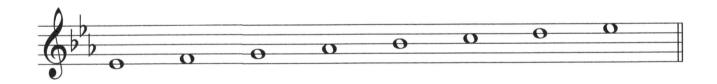

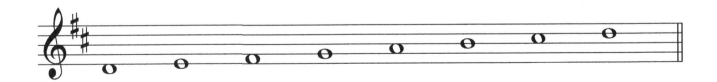

Chords

2. Write the following solid triads using key signatures. Add functional and root/quality chord symbols to each.

The tonic triad of C major	The dominant triad of E♭ major	The subdominant triad of D major	The tonic triad of F major
The dominant triad of A major	The tonic triad of B♭ major	The subdominant triad of C major	The dominant triad of G major
The tonic triad of G major	The dominant triad of B♭ major	The subdominant triad of F major	The tonic triad of A major

3. For the following triads: Name the major key. Identify the triad as tonic, subdominant, or dominant. Write the root/quality chord symbols for each.

Key: _____ _____ _____ _____
Triad: _____ _____ _____ _____

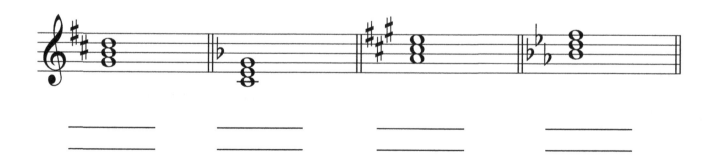

_____ _____ _____ _____

_____ _____ _____ _____

Chords

Minor Triads

Minor triads are considered "minor" because they are made up of specific intervals.

A minor triad consists of a minor third and a perfect fifth above the root.

Figure 10.3 contains a minor triad built on the root D. There is a minor third between D and F and a perfect fifth between D and A. All minor triads contain these intervals between the root and third and the root and fifth.

Figure 10.3

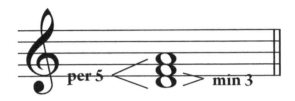

D - F = minor 3rd
D - A = perfect 5th

Triads in Minor Keys

Triads built on $\hat{1}$, $\hat{4}$, and $\hat{5}$ of the harmonic minor scale result in two minor triads (tonic and subdominant) and one major triad (dominant). The dominant triad contains raised $\hat{7}$ and is a major triad. For now, we will always use the harmonic form of the minor scale with raised $\hat{7}$ when building the dominant triad in the minor key.

Figure 10.4 contains the triads built on $\hat{1}$, $\hat{4}$, and $\hat{5}$ in D minor. Functional chord symbols for minor chords use lower case Roman numerals (i, iv). Root/quality symbols for minor chords use the letter name of the root with an "m" beside it to indicate minor (Dm, Gm). Some books use 'min' for minor chords (Dmin, Gmin)

Figure 10.4

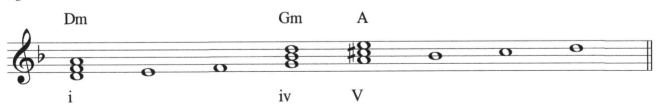

Chords

1. Write triads on $\hat{1}$, $\hat{4}$, and $\hat{5}$ of the following harmonic minor scales. Add the functional and the root/quality chord symbols.

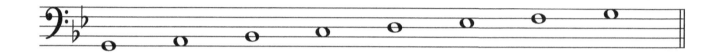

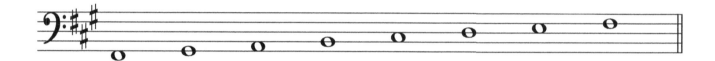

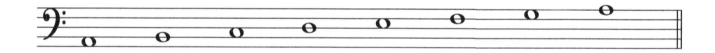

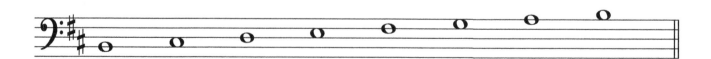

Chords

2. Write the following solid triads using key signatures. Add functional and root/quality chord symbols to each.

The tonic triad of D minor	The dominant triad of G minor	The subdominant triad of C minor	The tonic triad of A minor

The dominant triad of B minor	The tonic triad of F♯ minor	The subdominant triad of E minor	The dominant triad of E minor

The tonic triad of C minor	The dominant triad of F♯ minor	The subdominant triad of D minor	The tonic triad of E minor

3. For the following triads: Name the minor key. Identify the triad as tonic, subdominant, or dominant. Write the functional chord symbols for each.

Key: _____ _____ _____ _____
Triad: _____ _____ _____ _____

_____ _____ _____ _____
_____ _____ _____ _____

Chords

11
Melody

Review - The Motive

A *motive* is a short melodic idea that may be repeated higher or lower. This repetition of a musical idea at a higher or lower pitch is called a *sequence*. In Figure 11.1 the melodic motive is repeated three times, descending by the interval of a third each time.

Figure 11.1

Ludwig van Beethoven
Sonatina in F major

1. Identify the motives and sequences in the following melodies.

Christian Petzold
Minuet in G major

Johann Baptist Vaňhal
Sonatine 6, II

Melodic Movement

Most melodies contain three different types of motion (Figure 11.2):

1. **Conjunct motion** which is stepwise movement.
2. **Disjunct motion** which is movement by leap. A leap is the interval of a 3rd or larger.
3. **Repetition**.

Most good melodies are a combination of some or all of these types of movement. A melody should have a sense of shape or direction. A melody often rises to a high point, or climax, and then moves down again. Motion by step is most common.

Study the motion in Figure 11.2. The movement is indicated with brackets. 1. for conjunct, 2. for disjunct, and 3. for repetition.

Figure 11.2

2. Identify and bracket the movement in the following melodies as: 1. Conjunct, 2. Disjunct, or 3. Repetition.

Melody

Melodic Leaps

Leaps are an important part of melody writing. A leap is considered the interval of a 3rd or larger. Leaps within a melody have to be treated carefully. They add interest and contrast, but too many leaps may cause a melody to lose its shape. Instrumental melodies are often different than vocal melodies since the range and abilities of certain instruments are greater than those of the human voice. The treatment of leaps is an important element in good melody writing.

Figure 11.3 shows the treatment of some basic leaps. a) A leap of a 3rd is the smallest leap. After a leap of a 3rd a melody can proceed in any direction. For now, leaps larger than a 3rd like a 4th, 5th, 6th and octave should be followed by step or skip in the opposite direction. The leaps in b), c), and d) are approached and left by step in the opposite direction. **Don't leap the interval of a 7th.**

Figure 11.3

Sometimes more than one leap in a row can be effective. Two leaps in the same direction are acceptable if the intervals combine to form a chord.

Figure 11.4 a) contains two leaps that outline the C major triad. This is good. The leaps in b) work well because they outline a G major triad. The leaps in c) also work because they are notes of the C major triad. Two leaps adding up to the interval of a 7th are poor and should be avoided. In d) the two leaps add up to a 7th and don't outline any chord. This is poor.

Figure 11.4

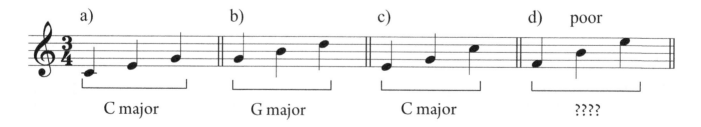

Repeated notes are effective, but too many can create melody that doesn't go anywhere.

Figure 11.5 has too many D's and C's. This is a boring melody that doesn't have any direction.

Figure 11.5

D major

The highest note of a melody can be a climax or high point.

In Figure 11.6, the highest note B♭ appears once and acts as a climax for the melody. The melody moves up to B♭, and then back down to the tonic E♭ in a classic arch shape. This is effective, but not always necessary. Every melody has its own unique character. Different techniques can be used when writing a melody depending on the mood or character that you want to convey.

Figure 11.6

The British Grenadiers
16th century

E♭ major

The melody in Figure 11.7 is a good melody. It contains a motive in measure one that is repeated one step higher in measure two. The leap of a 6th is left with stepwise motion in the opposite direction. The melody ends on the tonic which is the most stable pitch. $\hat{1}$ and $\hat{3}$ are stable pitches. $\hat{2}$ and $\hat{7}$ are unstable pitches. It is very effective to end a melody on the tonic ($\hat{1}$), approached from a step above ($\hat{2}$ - $\hat{1}$), or from a half step below ($\hat{7}$ - $\hat{1}$).

Figure 11.7

D major

Melody

1. Compose a melody in G major, using a combination of steps, skips and leaps, ending on a stable pitch. Use the given rhythm. The melodic motive under the bracket should be repeated in the second measure, starting on a different pitch.

G major

2. Compose a melody in E♭ major, using a combination of steps, skips and leaps, ending on a stable pitch. Use the given rhythm. The melodic motive under the bracket should be repeated in the second measure, starting on a different pitch.

E♭ major

3. Compose a melody in A major, using a combination of steps, skips and leaps, ending on a stable pitch. Use the given rhythm. The melodic motive under the bracket should be repeated in the second measure, starting on a different pitch.

A major

4. Compose a melody in D major, using a combination of steps, skips and leaps, ending on a stable pitch. Use the given rhythm. Write a a motive in measure one and repeat it in the second measure, starting on a different pitch.

5. Compose a melody in B♭ major, using a combination of steps, skips and leaps, ending on a stable pitch. Use the given rhythm. Write a a motive in measure one and repeat it in the second measure, starting on a different pitch.

6. Compose a melody in C major, using a combination of steps, skips and leaps, ending on a stable pitch. Use the given rhythm. Write a a motive in measure one and repeat it in the second measure, starting on a different pitch.

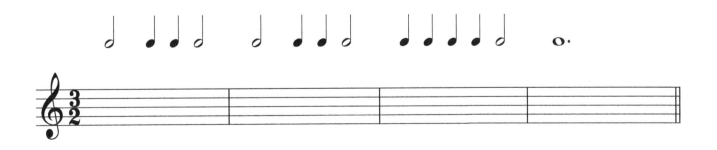

Melody

12
History 3

Piotr Ilyich Tchaikovsky (1840 - 1893) Romantic Era

Piotr Ilyich Tchaikovsky was born in Votkinsk, a town in Russia's Ural Mountains. His father was a Ukrainian mining engineer. He began piano lessons when he was five years old. In 1850 he moved to the city of St. Petersburg. Here, Tchaikovsky studied law because music was not considered an acceptable profession.

While in law school, Tchaikovsky continued to study music. He attended the opera and theater with his classmates. At age 23 he gave up his legal job with the Ministry of Justice and went to study music full time at the St. Petersburg Conservatory. In 1863, he moved to Moscow, where he became a professor of harmony at the Moscow Conservatory. It is now named after him.

Tchaikovsky wrote six symphonies, the famous Piano Concerto in B♭ major, a handful of operas and three ballets of which, "Swan Lake," "The Nutcracker" and "Sleeping Beauty" are his most famous works. During his life, his music was extremely popular, and he was in great demand as a conductor.

For many years, Tchaikovsky had a patroness named Nadezhda von Meck -- a wealthy widow who supported the arts and artists. She sent him money monthly so that he could concentrate on composing without having to worry about making a living. For 14 years they communicated by letter, but von Meck insisted that they never meet in person. Tchaikovsky dedicated his Fourth Symphony to her.

Tchaikovsky traveled all over Europe for performances of his music. In 1891, he went to America where he was invited to conduct the New York Symphony at the opening of Carnegie Hall.

He died in St. Petersburg on November 6, 1893. The cause of his death was officially declared as cholera; an infection usually contracted from drinking dirty or contaminated water.

The Nutcracker

Piotr Ilyich Tchaikovsky's ballet, *The Nutcracker*, written in 1892, is based on a story by German author E.T.A. Hoffmann. The ballet was choreographed by Marius Petipa and Lev Ivanov. A choreographer designs the dances for a ballet.

In The Nutcracker, a Christmas present, a nutcracker, comes to life as a handsome prince. He takes the young girl who received him as a present on some fantastic adventures. This is one of Tchaikovsky's most famous compositions, and perhaps the most popular ballet in the world.

This is a summary of the story of The Nutcracker.

Act I

It is Christmas Eve and Dr. Stahlbaum and his wife, a former ballerina, are giving a party. Their children, Clara and Fritz, are happy to see the guests. All of the children are given toys. The mysterious Dr. Drosselmeyer is at the party, and performs magic tricks for the children. Dr. Drosselmeyer gives Clara a Nutcracker. She is fascinated by it, and she believes that it has magical powers. Fritz breaks the Nutcracker, and it mysteriously fixes itself. The party comes to an end, the guests depart and the family goes to bed.

Clara is restless and cannot sleep. She sneaks downstairs looking for the Nutcracker. At the stroke of midnight, strange things begin to happen. The room fills with giant mice who attack Clara. The Nutcracker, leading an army of life-size toy soldiers, come to Clara's rescue. The Rat King, who is the leader of the mice attacks the Nutcracker, and Clara hits him with her shoe. The Nutcracker wins the battle and is transformed into a handsome prince.

The Nutcracker Prince turns Clara's house into the Land of Snow. The Snow Queen and the Nutcracker Prince dance with the Snowflakes. Clara and the Nutcracker Prince depart for the Kingdom of Sweets in an enchanted sleigh.

Act II

Clara and the Nutcracker Prince travel across the Lemonade Sea to the beautiful Land of Sweets, ruled by the Sugar Plum Fairy. At the Kingdom of Sweets, the cooks are preparing delicious treats for their visit. The Sugar Plum Fairy welcomes them to her kingdom. In Clara's honor, the Sugar Plum Fairy has her subjects dance for them while they eat. After, the Sugar Plum Fairy and the Nutcracker Prince dance a grand pas de deux.

As the celebration concludes, Clara drifts off to sleep. She awakens at home, but it appears all this was just a dream. Christmas Eve is over. Clara, still thinking of the marvelous dream, is sitting at home by the Christmas tree, with the Nutcracker-Doll on her lap.

Waltz of the Flowers and Dance of the Sugar Plum Fairy

The "Waltz of the Flowers" is a piece from the second act of The Nutcracker. This is one of Tchaikovsky's most well-known compositions. It has been performed and arranged for many combinations of instruments and instrumental groups.

The "Dance of the Sugar Plum Fairy" is a dance from Act 2 of the Nutcracker. The Sugar Plum Fairy dances a pas de deux with her prince. A pas de deux is a dance duet in which two dancers, typically a male and a female, perform ballet steps together. This dance was choreographed by Lev Ivanov.

Choreographer Marius Petipa envisioned the Sugar Plum Fairy's music sounding like "drops of water shooting from a fountain." To achieve this, Tchaikovsky used an instrument called a **celesta**. The celesta looks a little like a piano but has metal plates instead of strings. The plates are hit by hammers, producing a soft, bell-like sound. Tchaikovsky wrote, "The celesta is midway between a tiny piano and a Glockenspiel, with a divinely wonderful sound."

The "Dance of the Sugar Plum Fairy" is one of the ballet's best known musical works.

Music Terms

Review the following musical terms from Levels 1 to 4 that are related to tempo.

accelerando, accel	becoming quicker
adagio	a slow tempo between andante and largo
allegretto	fairly fast, a little slower than allegro
allegro	fast
lento	slow
moderato	at a moderate tempo
presto	very fast
prestissimo	as fast as possible
rallentando	slowing down
ritardando	slowing down gradually
tempo	speed at which music is performed
Tempo primo, Tempo I	return to the original tempo
vivace	lively, brisk

History 3

13
Music Analysis

Form in Music

Music is often organized into sections. The general organization of these sections is called **form**. The form of a piece of music demonstrates its structure and can help the listener relate to and understand the intentions of the composer.

One way to approach music composition is through form. A composer uses phrases to represent musical ideas. The phrases are like musical sentences that make up the sections of a composition. Like sentences in a story, the individual phrases work together to create a complete paragraph and contribute to the larger musical section. Phrases are typically four measures long and often end on a longer note or a rest. This acts like the period of a sentence, giving a small pause between each phrase.

Phrases help to create sections in music. Composers may write phrases in groups that work together to form a section of music or an entire composition. We can label these phrases with letters to help identify the form and structure.

Study the phrases in Figure 13.1.

Phrase 1:

The letter '*a*' is used to identify the first phrase (mm.1 - 4) and any other phrases that are exactly the same. This phrase ends on scale degree $\hat{5}$, making it feel unfinished. It is four measures long and ends on a half note, giving pause before the next phrase begins.

Phrase 2:

The second phrase (mm.5 - 8) acts as a resolution or answer to the first phrase. It is labeled '*a*¹.' '*a*¹' is used to label phrases that are very similar to '*a*' but may contain some slight differences. This phrase is the same as '*a*' except for the last note. It is four measures long and ends on a stable pitch ($\hat{1}$). It also ends with a rest, giving pause before the next section starts.

Music Analysis

Phrase 3:

The third phrase (mm. 9 - 12) is labeled '*b*' because the melody is different than phrase '*a*.' Music needs **repetition** so the listener has something familiar to hear, but it also needs **contrast** so it does not become boring. The two elements work together to make great compositions. If '*a*' was stated three times in a row, it might become too repetitive. This new material provides diversity and contrast. Phrase 3 is four measures long and ends on an unstable pitch ($\hat{5}$).

Phrase 4:

The fourth phrase (mm.13 - 16) is the same as phrase two, and like phrase two, it is labelled '*a¹*.' This phrase rounds out the piece and it ends on a stable pitch.

Figure 13.1

Cornelius Gurlitt
Vivace, Op. 117, No. 8

Music Analysis

1. Answer the questions dealing with the following compositions.

Franz Schubert
Slumber Song

a. Add the time signature directly on the music.

b. Name the key of this piece. _____

c. Mark the phrases with slurs.

d. Label the phrases with *a*, *a*[1], and *b*.

e. Name the chord formed by the notes at A: _____ B: _____

Music Analysis

Piano Sonata, Mvt. I

Franz Joseph Haydn
(1732-1809)

Presto

a. Add the correct time signature directly on the music.

b. Name the key of this piece._____

c. Name the composer of this piece. _____

d. On which beat does this piece begin? _____

e. Name the intervals at : A_____ B _____ C _____

f. Does this piece end on a stable or unstable degree? _____

g. Explain the sign at D _____

h. Define *Presto* _____

i. Find one half step and circle it.

Music Analysis

Menuetto

Wolfgang Amadeus Mozart
(1756-1791)

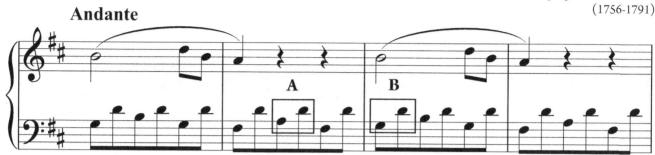

a. Add the correct time signature directly on the music.

b. Name the key of this piece._____

c. Name the composer of this piece. _____

d. When did this composer live? _____

e. Name the intervals at : A_____ B _____ C _____

f. Explain the sign at D _____

h. Define *andante* _____

i. Does this piece end on a stable or unstable scale degree? _____

j. Name the triad formed by the notes at E: _____

k. In this key, this triad is the: ❏ tonic triad   ❏ subdominant triad   ❏ dominant triad

Music Analysis

Review 3

1. Write the following solid triads using key signatures. Add functional and root/quality chord symbols to each.

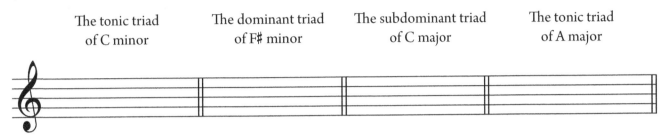

The tonic triad of C minor	The dominant triad of F♯ minor	The subdominant triad of C major	The tonic triad of A major

The dominant triad of G minor	The tonic triad of D minor	The subdominant triad of B♭ major	The dominant triad of E♭ major

2. For the following triads: Name the major key. Identify the triad as tonic, subdominant, or dominant. Write the functional chord symbols under each chord.

Key: _____   _____   _____   _____
Triad: _____   _____   _____   _____

3. For the following triads: Name the minor key. Identify the triad as tonic, subdominant, or dominant. Write the root/quality chord symbols above each chord.

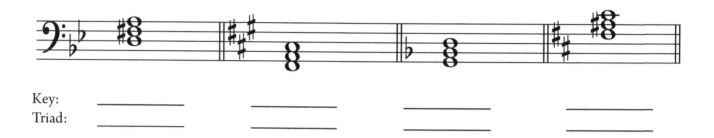

Key: _____   _____   _____   _____
Triad: _____   _____   _____   _____

4. Compose a melody in B♭ major, using a combination of steps, skips and leaps, ending on a stable pitch. Use the given rhythm. The melodic motive under the bracket should be repeated in the second measure, starting on a different pitch.

5. Compose a melody in E♭ major, using a combination of steps, skips and leaps, ending on a stable pitch. Use the given rhythm. Write a a motive in measure one and repeat it in the second measure, starting on a different pitch.

6. Answer the following questions.

a. Who composed *The Nutcracker*? _____

b. In what country was he born? _____

c. In what era did he live? _____

d. How many symphonies did he write? _____

e. What type of work is *The Nutcracker*? _____

f. Name a dance from *The Nutcracker*. _____

g. Who choreographed *The Nutcracker*?

                1. _____

                2. _____

h. What is a choreographer? _____

_____

i. What unique instrument is featured in *The Nutcracker*? _____

7. Match the following musical terms with their definitions

_____ *cantabile*   a) becoming quicker

_____ *vivace*   b) a slow tempo between andante and largo

_____ *rallentando*   c) fairly fast, a little slower than allegro

_____ *dolce*   d) fast

_____ *marcato*   e) slow

_____ *Tempo primo*   f) at a moderate tempo

_____ *adagio*   g) very fast

_____ *ritardando*   h) as fast as possible

_____ *allegretto*   i) slowing down

_____ *prestissimo*   j) slowing down gradually

_____ *grazioso*   k) speed at which music is performed

_____ *moderato*   l) return to the original tempo

_____ *presto*   m) lively, brisk

_____ *accelerando*   n) in a singing style

_____ *maestoso*   o) sweetly

_____ *tempo*   p) gracefully

_____ *allegro*   q) majestically

_____ *lento*   r) marked or stressed

Music Terms and Signs

Terms

accelerando, accel.	becoming quicker
accent	a stressed note
adagio	slow
allegretto	fairly fast, a little slower than allegro
allegro	fast
andante	moderately slow, at a walking pace
a tempo	return to the original tempo
cantabile	in a singing style
crescendo, cresc.	becoming louder
da capo, D.C.	from the beginning
D.C. al fine	repeat from the beginning and end at *Fine*
dal segno, D.S. 𝄋	from the sign
decrescendo, decresc.	becoming softer
diminuendo, dim.	becoming softer
dolce	sweetly, gentle
fine	the end
forte, f	loud
fortissimo, ff	very loud
grazioso	gracefully
legato	smooth
lento	slow
maestoso	majestically
mano destra, m.d.	right hand
mano sinistra, m.s.	left hand

marcato	play marked or stressed
mezzo forte, mf	moderately loud
mezzo piano, mp	moderately soft
moderato	at a moderate tempo
molto	much, very
ottava, 8va	the interval of an octave
pianissimo, pp	very soft
piano, p	soft
poco	little
prestissimo	as fast as possible
presto	very fast
rallentando, rall.	slowing down
ritardando, rit.	slowing down gradually
staccato	play short and detached
tempo	speed at which music is performed
Tempo Primo, Tempo I	return to the original tempo
vivace	lively, brisk

Music Terms and Signs

Signs

accent - a stressed note

common time - symbol for 4/4

crescendo - becoming louder

decrescendo - becoming softer

double bar line - the end of a piece

fermata - hold note or rest longer than written value

slur - play the notes smoothly (legato)

staccato - play short and detached

tie - hold for the combined value of the tied notes

repeat marks - at the second sign go back to the first sign and repeat the music from there. The first sign is left out if the music is repeated from the beginning.

tenuto mark - when placed over or under a note, hold it for its full value.

pedal symbol - press/release the right pedal.

Music Terms and Signs

dal segno, D.S. - from the sign.

 **8va** - play one octave higher than written pitch.

 **8va** - play one octave lower than written pitch.

 down bow - on a string instrument, play the note by drawing the bow downward.

 up bow - on a string instrument, play the note by drawing the bow upward.

breath mark - take a breath or a small break

Music Terms and Signs

Made in the USA
Middletown, DE
02 October 2023

39981805R00053